SUPERMOO!

Babette Cole

MAMMOTH

Most people think cows are
boring old munchers . . .

Well, this one isn't . . .

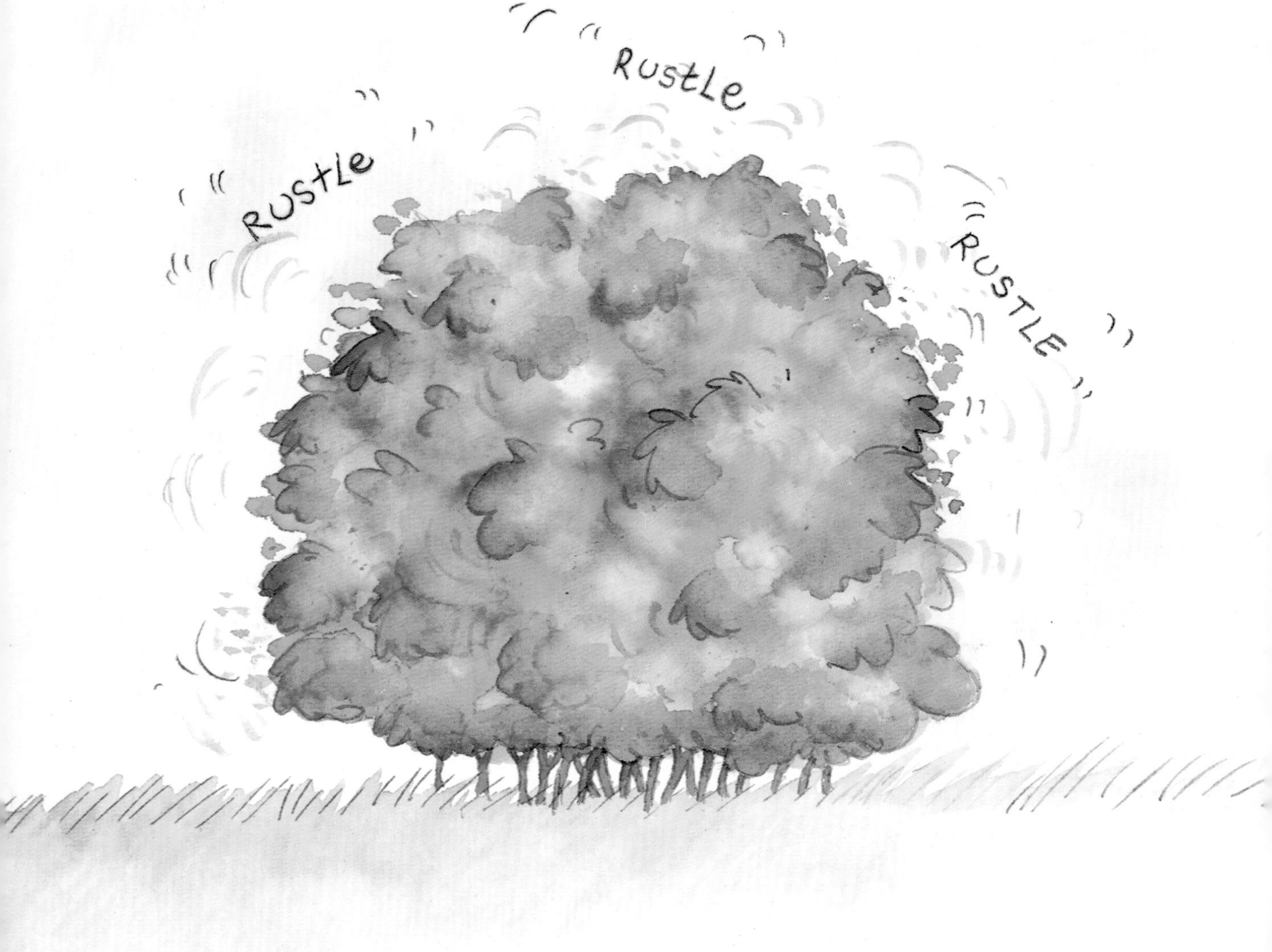
RUSTLE
RUSTLE
RUSTLE

This is
SUPERMOO!

Down in the Cowcave her friend,
Calf Crypton, works
the cowputer.

When there is a world disaster they
are the first to know.
"Crikey cream cheese!" said Calf Crypton.
"This message is
important!"

When Supermoo was plugged into the cowputer her supervision could flash up what was happening.
"Suffering silage," said Supermoo, "it's the devilish **BOTS!**"

There was no time to lose!
They sped out to sea.

The Bots, evil spreaders of filth and pollution, were making a smelly fog with their Bot pipes.

The fog caused two treacle tankers to smack into each other. There was treacle everywhere!

Supermoo bashed the Bots.

"Keep our country green and clean, you dirty things!" said Supermoo.

Supermoo and Calf Crypton saved the crews
by picking up the tankers with their
magnetic hoofs.

They zoomed towards the shore.

They flew the tankers to the docks
to be mended.

On the beach, Miss Pimple's class was having a swimming lesson.

The treacle slick from the crash was coming straight for them!

Supermoo blew
a huge
bubble.

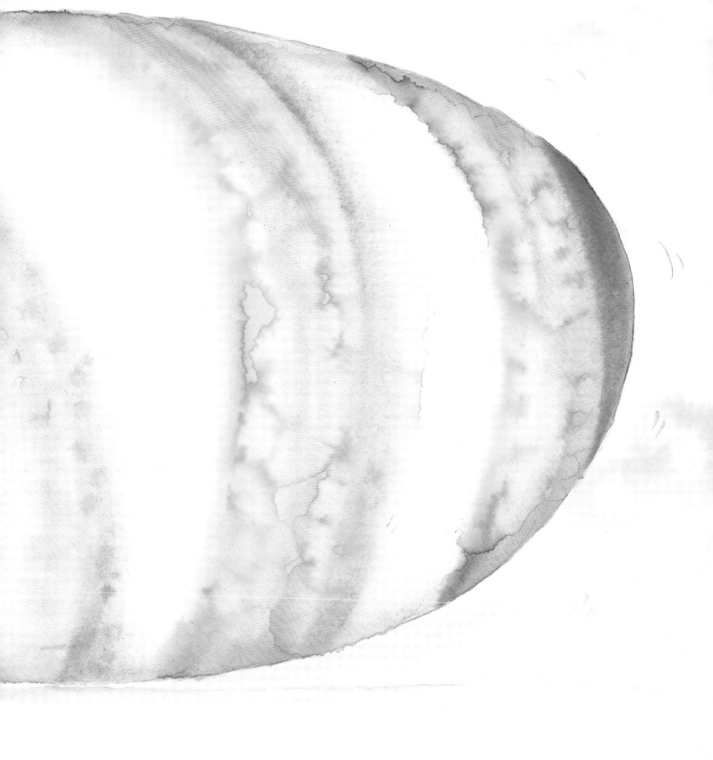

They rolled the bubble in
the treacle.

All the treacle stuck to it.
Supermoo and
Calf Crypton
carried it
away.

Miss Pimple's class was saved!

Then a message came through on
their electronic ear-pieces.
It was from the
United
Nations!

"Frying flies!" said Supermoo.

An oil-well was on fire and had
to be put out.

Supermoo and Calf Crypton flew the
treacle bubble towards
the blazing well.

When they were over
the well Supermoo
popped the bubble
with her horns.

All the treacle
went down the well
and put out the fire.

It was so hot it turned into a giant toffee tube.

Miss Pimple's class had toffee
for ever.

"Put the paper in a bin," said Supermoo.

On the way home someone called them with the "Cowsign".
Could it be another cowbusting crime to crack . . . ?

No! It was time
to deliver the
milk . . .

. . . in the Cowmobile!

First published in Great Britain 1992
by BBC Books
Published 1994 by Mammoth
an imprint of Reed Consumer Books Ltd
Michelin House, 81 Fulham Road, London SW3 6RB
and Auckland, Melbourne, Singapore and Toronto

10 9 8 7 6 5 4 3 2

Copyright © Babette Cole 1992

ISBN 0 7497 1245 7

A CIP catalogue record for this title
is available from the British Library

Produced by Mandarin Offset Ltd
Printed and bound in Hong Kong

This paperback is sold subject to the condition
that it shall not, by way of trade or otherwise,
be lent, resold, hired out, or otherwise circulated
without the publisher's prior consent in any form
of binding or cover other than that in which
it is published and without a similar condition
including this condition being imposed
on the subsequent purchaser.